# Goldilocks and the Three Bears

Once upon a time, there lived a family of three bears in a cozy cottage in the woods. Papa Bear, Mama Bear, and little Baby Bear led a peaceful life in their secluded home.

One morning, Mama Bear returned home from an early trip to the market with a basket of fresh apples. Papa Bear and Baby Bear greeted her outdoors. Everyone was eager for breakfast.

Mama Bear had prepared porridge, and now it was ready to eat. As she served them each their portion, the porridge steamed. It was much too hot!

The Bears decided to take a walk while their porridge cooled.

Meanwhile, a curious blond-haired girl named Goldilocks was wandering alone through the woods. She saw the Bears' cottage and wondered what lay inside. She decided to get a closer look.

She walked right up and knocked on the door. When there was no answer, she went inside. There were three bowls of porridge on the kitchen table.

Goldilocks was hungry. She grabbed a spoon and took a mouthful from the big bowl.

"This porridge is too hot!" she wailed.

She moved on to the second bowl, which wasn't any better.

"This porridge is too cold!" she complained.

The hungry little girl had a spoonful from the smallest bowl.

"Yum!" she announced with relief. "This porridge is just right!"

Goldilocks gobbled up the porridge until the bowl was empty.

Next, Goldilocks wandered into a cozy, inviting den and saw three chairs. A book lay on the biggest chair, a basket of yarn and knitting needles were beside the middle-sized chair, and there were some toys on the floor next to the smallest chair of all. After having wandered through the woods, Goldilocks was eager to rest her tired feet.

Goldilocks climbed onto the biggest chair with great difficulty.

"This chair is too high," she said. "My feet don't even touch the ground!"

Next, she tried sitting on the medium-sized chair. It looked like it would be a better fit and was also more lady-like. But it was no good either!

"Oh dear, this chair is also too big!" she sighed, trying to find a comfortable spot.

Then, Goldilocks turned to the smallest chair. She eased into it and smiled.

"This chair is just right," she said with relief.

Suddenly, Goldilocks heard the chair's legs creak beneath her. Crash! The chair fell apart and Goldilocks ended up on the floor!

"Oops," she said sheepishly.

Goldilocks was getting tired and sleepy from all of the excitement.
She spotted a staircase, and was curious to see where it led to.
She wandered upstairs and saw three well-made beds in a sunny loft.

"I just need to lie down for a minute," Goldilocks yawned.

The biggest bed with the heavy oak headboard looked like the perfect place to rest. She hoisted herself up and nestled under the covers. But it wasn't what she expected.

"This bed is too hard!" she grumbled.

Goldilocks hopped down and shuffled over to the medium-sized frilly pink bed in the middle. This had to be it!

"This bed is too soft!" she hollered.

After struggling to get out of the second bed, Goldilocks climbed into the little bed with the teddy bear on top of it. By now, she was certainly tired!

"This bed is just right…" she murmured as she fell into a deep sleep.

While she was sleeping, the Bears came home from their walk to find the front door of the cottage slightly ajar. Papa Bear took a cautious look around and immediately sensed that something was wrong.

"Someone has been in the house!" he exclaimed.

Papa Bear entered the cottage first.

"Who could it be, Papa?" wondered Baby Bear.

Mama Bear and Baby Bear hung back until Papa Bear glanced around and waved them inside.

Mama Bear rushed into the kitchen. She gasped when she saw the sloppy porridge bowls on the table.

"Someone's been eating my porridge!" she shrieked.

"Someone's been eating my porridge!" Papa Bear yelled.

"Someone's been eating my porridge, too," sulked Baby Bear. "And it's all gone!"

The Bears walked carefully toward the den.

"Someone's been sitting in my chair!" Papa Bear growled.

"Someone's been sitting in my chair!" Mama Bear yelped.

"Someone's been sitting in my chair, too," cried Baby Bear, picking up a chair leg. "And now it's broken!"

Papa Bear led the family quietly up the stairs. They knew something was fishy as soon as they saw that the bedsheets were wrinkled.

"Someone's been sleeping in my bed!" Papa Bear roared.

"Someone's been sleeping in my bed!" Mama Bear wailed.

"S-s-someone's been s-s-sleeping in my bed, t-t-too," stuttered Baby Bear. "And she's still there!"

Goldilocks stretched and yawned.

Papa Bear, Mama Bear, and Baby Bear all gathered around Baby Bear's bed and peered at the waking girl.

Goldilocks rolled over and opened her eyes. Staring back at her were three bewildered bears.

"Yikes!" she gasped. What a surprise!

Everyone was quite startled as they all looked back at each other.

Goldilocks leaped out of bed in a flash. The Bears watched as she bolted down the stairs and through the door, and ran all the way home.

"I guess she didn't want to stay and visit," Papa Bear muttered.

Once she was a fair distance away, Goldilocks glanced back at the cottage in the woods.

"That was close," she huffed.

From that day on, Goldilocks vowed not to let her curiosity get the better of her and to put an end to her snooping. The Bears never saw their golden-haired visitor ever again.